The Man Who Lived Backwards and Other Stories

Nodens Chapbooks:

Sable Revery: Poems, Sketches, Letters, by Robert Nelson

The Ghost in the Tower: Sketches of Lost Jacobia, by Earl H.
   Reed

The Man Who Lived Backwards and Other Stories, by Charles
   F. Hall

The Man Who Lived Backwards and Other Stories

by

Charles F. Hall

Nodens Chapbooks
2017

The Man Who Lived Backwards and Other Stories

Nodens Chapbooks no. 3

First published by Nodens Books, 2017
This edition copyright © Nodens Books, L.L.C.
Cover art by Harry Turner.
ISBN 9781976499418
Printed in the United States of America
First edition: October 2017

Nodens Books   www.nodensbooks.com
PO Box 493
Marcellus, MI 49067

Acknowledgements

Several people helped me research Charles F. Hall, and I'm grateful to Mike Ashley, Ned Brooks, Joe R. Christopher, Alistair Durie, Andrew Higgins, Dale Nelson, and Andrew Parry.

Table of Contents

Introduction

In 1938 a young British writer named Charles F. Hall published three science fiction stories, and then disappeared without a trace. He has long been presumed an early casualty of World War II. But his first story has gained a small reputation because C.S. Lewis read it and was influenced by it. In the preface to *The Great Divorce* (1946), Lewis wrote: "I must acknowledge my debt to a writer whose name I have forgotten and whom I read several years ago in a highly coloured American magazine of what they call 'scientifiction'. The unbendable and unbreakable quality of my heavenly matter was suggested to me by him, though he used the fancy for a different and most ingenious purpose. His hero traveled into the past and there very properly found raindrops that would pierce him like bullets and sandwiches that no strength would bite because, of course, nothing in the past can be altered. I, with less originality, but I hope with equal propriety, have transferred this to the eternal. If the writer of that story ever reads these lines I ask him to accept my grateful acknowledgement."

It was many years before this unnamed story by an unremembered author was located. I learned of it from the late Ned Brooks, who also sent me a copy of the story. Thus I was able to reprint it in my anthology *Tales Before Narnia* (2008). At that time, only a second story by Hall was known, but later Mike Ashley discovered a third. This volume collects for the first time all three of Hall's short stories—in fact, Hall's entire known output.

As I remarked in the headnote to "The Man Who Live Backwards" in *Tales Before Narnia*, Lewis was wrong about the story appearing in an American magazine. It appeared in a short-lived, highly colored British science fiction magazine titled *Tales of Wonder*, edited by Walter H. Gillings. *Tales of Wonder* published sixteen issues between 1937 and 1942. "The Man Who Lived Backwards" appeared in issue no. 3 (Summer 1938), and a second tale by Hall, "The Time-Drug," appeared in issue no. 5 (Winter 1938).

Hall's third story, "Paid without Protest," appeared in the 8 October 1938 issue of the non-genre magazine *The Passing Show* (v. 7 no. 342), where it was signed "C.F. Hall." That this is the same author is evidenced in the November 1938 issue of *Novae Terrae*, the first British science fiction fanzine, where it refers to Hall as "author of [the] hit story 'The Man Who Lived Backwards'" and notes that the new story is about "an apparent television-phone" (p. 25).

About the only biographical information that has been found about Hall is in the Spring 1938 issue of *Tomorrow*, where it says that "A new British author whose work promises to be immediately popular appears in the person of C.F. Hall, a member of B.I.S., who contributes 'The Man Who Lived Backwards' as his first published story" (p. 6). The B.I.S. is the British Interplanetary Society, but a perusal of their journal from the 1930s and 40s gives no mentions of Hall, who remains an enigma, the author of three known short stories, one of which has brought Hall's work some notice for its influence on C.S. Lewis.

Douglas A. Anderson

The Man Who Lived Backwards
and Other Stories

The Man Who Lived Backwards

THE DISAPPEARANCE

The case of Nicolai Rostof was bewildering enough in its confirmed facts, without taking into account his personal narrative. With regard to the latter, the public immediately hailed him as a modern Baron Münchhausen, news reporters as a heaven-sent opportunity for a farcical write-up, and scientists as a maundering lunatic.

That is where I think the little man was done a grave injustice. For the Press, seizing on his story as an incredible explanation of an even more incredible situation, wrote it up in the way it always does in such cases—as a huge joke. The public, gulping its morning coffee and bacon, shuffled blindly after the leader-writers' pipings and started a great big laugh that echoed from Peckham to Kamschatka; and that, of course, made any scientist who might have thought of starting a serious investigation shy clear of the whole affair like a frightened horse.

I am not a scientist—not in the physics line, at any rate; but I have had twenty years' experience as a practising psychologist, and I will stake my life on this: Rostof believed every word of his account was true, believed that the whole amazing sequence of events had actually happened to him, no matter what other explanation may be offered.

If we stop to consider his story logically and dispassionately, together with the known facts, instead of indulging in mere cachinnation, the disquieting thought comes to us that there is no known law which says it could *not* have happened. You may assert that Rostof cannot prove his story, but at least you can't *dis*prove it.

Nicolai Rostof, dark, inoffensive and five-foot-six, was physics and chemistry master at Gayling Grammar School. He had no relations in England, but he had two friends, one Hans Schouten, a Dutchman, and the other Harold Matheson, history-master at the Grammar School. These three had a common interest which brought them together at leisure-time in a hut on some waste land on the outskirts of Gayling.

They were all interested in modern experimental physics, and had got together a rough, but fairly efficient laboratory in which they were trying to duplicate and extend some of Lord Rutherford's experiments in the transmutation of elements. In connection with this, at the time, they were studying the effect of high-frequency, high-voltage electrical discharges—"miniature lightning flashes of a million volts," to use Rostof's words.

On Tuesday, January 20th, at 3 p.m., Rostof was on the platform of his classroom in the Grammar School taking the third form. He was standing in full view away from his desk; he did not seem in any way unusual in manner or state of mind. There was not the slightest warning that anything out of the ordinary was about to occur. Yet, as he was tapping the blackboard with his pointer, demonstrating some point, something happened to him which startled his politely blank faced class far more than if he had stood on his head and screamed.

He disappeared.

No sound; no flash—nothing. . . . Only thirty-two round-eyed, open-mouthed boys staring at an empty platform.

It says much for the impression which the incident made upon them that they sat in silence for fully three minutes before one or two older boys made a tentative search, and finally went for the head-master.

But the most painstaking scrutiny by a combined force of masters and prefects revealed only one thing: that the science-master had vanished in a split second from Gayling Grammar School.

The third form meanwhile found its voice and discussed the miracle from every conceivable angle, though the only explanation meeting with almost general agreement came from a golden-haired infant who darkly hinted that the devil had claimed his own.

To suggest that the whole of these thirty-two witnesses were hypnotised is going a little too far. Besides, the masters were certainly not hypnotised; and as Matheson confided to me when talking over the case afterwards, "Anyone who thinks he can hypnotise those young devils had never had any experience of Gayling Grammar scholars."

ROSTOF'S STORY

As you know, that wasn't the last that was seen of Rostof on that amazing Tuesday afternoon. For at precisely the same instant that he disappeared from his classroom platform, or as nearly as can be ascertained, he appeared out of the air in the grounds of Mrs. Van der Rorvik's stately house, approximately a mile and a half away from the grammar school.

A minor detail is that he had no slightest vestige of clothing on him.

The only witness to his coming in this case was the head gardener, a simple-minded man by the name of Curle, although the postman, in response to Curle's shout, caught sight of him about two minutes afterwards.

To see a man pop up out of nothingness in the middle of an empty lawn is not exactly a sedative for the nerves. Curle had been looking across the lawn toward the house, presumably turning over in his mind some manner of begonias or seedling stocks, when—*flick!* There was a naked man, staggering slightly, hair dishevelled, eyes staring wildly, a red scar on the whiteness of his shoulder and blood on his arm.

The gardener's natural alarm was increased by Rostof's first action which was to run towards him shouting the strange words: "Thank God it's stopped! You're moving right; you're moving right!"

Curle admits frankly that he thought he had to deal with a lunatic, and reached hurriedly for a spade, at the same time calling to the postman whom he had seen passing down the drive. Rostof, however, made no hostile act, but simply kept shaking the gardener's hand and babbling incoherently. On seeing him at closer quarters, Curle realised that the man was weak and exhausted; he had a two days' stubble of beard on his cheeks and his eyes were bloodshot.

With the arrival of the postman, Curle recovered some measure of his wits and took off his coat to drape about Rostof. Then together the two men led him to the doctor's house, which was fortunately only two doors away. As they went, Curle described the stranger's sudden appearance to the incredulous postman, though the manner of his appearance they could not explain.

Doctor Seebohm had the intelligence to see that Rostof was suffering from a severe shock and physical exhaustion, administered some restoratives and arranged for him to have two or three days in hospital. Not until then did he listen to Curle, and to Rostof's incoherent story.

As luck would have it, a *Gayling Guardian* reporter who was friendly with Seebohm was on the spot and scented a hot story. He took full notes, and the minute Rostof disappeared into the ambulance, acted swiftly. The result was that the morning papers trumpeted the whole story, although it was not until the next evening that it was connected with the Gayling Grammar School affair.

Those first accounts of Rostof's amazing experience were garbled in the extreme, and for the sake of clearness I will set down here, not the first disjointed recital, but the story as Rostof told it to me later, soberly and earnestly. It began with him being in the laboratory on the outskirts of Gayling at 6:30 p.m. on *Thursday, January 22nd.*

It was here that the public drew breath and let out its first great whoop of laughter. For on the Wednesday morning when the story appeared, Thursday simply hadn't been. It was to-morrow; it was the misty future; it was a dream more transient than a bursting bubble; and it smashed Rostof's reputation as a truthful man at the very start. But try to keep an open mind and listen to his story as he told it.

For he swore that on Tuesday, he had conducted his class without the slightest untoward incident. On Wednesday he had got up, shaved, breakfasted, gone through a normal school day, witnessed a fire at the Elite cinema at night, gone to bed; and so on again through Thursday until, at that fateful moment of half-past six, he was in the laboratory which he shared with Schouten and Matheson.

The other two were also there, in the main work-room, getting ready for a discharge which was to take place at seven. Schouten, who had no professional ties, had been there since three p.m., attending to the generators that were building up the charge in the great copper cone which hung four feet above the ground plate.

The discharge gap acted very much in the same manner as an ordinary simple spark-circuit works, with certain modifications due to size. A condenser, in which was stored the charge built up by the generators an enormous flat-ribbed inductance, and the gap itself, formed the major parts of the circuit. The break-down voltage across the gap was in the neighbourhood of 1,000,000 volts, and when the flash took place the condenser would empty and re-charge some thousands of times per second, in tune with the high-frequency oscillations.

THE OTHER ROSTOF

Rostof said that on the Thursday evening he had been in the small cubby-hole adjacent to the main room, where he had some short-wave radio apparatus. He had been listening-in for some twenty minutes, but got only poor results, due to very bad atmospherics, when he became aware that a freak thunderstorm was approaching outside. It was very unusual for the time of year, but there had been a spell of mild weather previously.

Anyhow, he gave up the radio as a bad job, got up and went into the next room. He had intended to hang his head-phones on their hook, and he pulled the terminals from their sockets for that purpose, but instead of bothering to go to the rack at that moment, kept hem on his head and slug the dangling leads over his shoulder.

He was surprised to find how dark it had grown when he entered the main laboratory, and realised that the storm must be much nearer than he had thought. He crossed toward the discharge gap with the intention of taking a look at the meters, and remembers Schouten making some warning remark about not touching the negative cone; though, of course, he new well enough himself not to touch any of the charged apparatus.

He went to take a look at the main volt-meter, and to see it behind its mica covering in the poor light he had to lean sideways and peer closely. The strain in the condensers and across the gap would then be roughly 850,000 volts.

As he bent, the loop of flex from the head-phones slipped from his shoulder and fell across the ground-plate, the tips of the metal terminals resting on the bare copper. Instantly he dropped a hand to switch them off, but before he could do so there came a blinding flare of light all about him and a stunning crash of sound.

He threw himself back, blinded and dazed. His first thought was that in some inconceivable manner the gap had shorted and he was electrocuted; but when he could think clearly he realised that the charge was not sufficient for a flash, and in any case, Schouten had not closed the switch which completed the circuit.

After a moment of blinking and a fleeting sensation of severe nausea had passed, he was surprised and relieved to find himself still alive. Surprisingly, too, the laboratory seemed to have suffered no damage; the gap was there, windows, apparatus, all unchanged, his friends bending over a bench. . . .

No; something was wrong! His clothes, the head-phones, had vanished completely. He stood agape with amazement beside the gleaming copper gap, stark naked.

For some time, he told me, he could do nothing but stand there like a village idiot, with staring eyes and hanging jaw. Helplessly he gazed around, as though the missing clothes might be dangling in mid-air, and as he did so he became aware that there was someone else in the room whom he had not noticed before. This was a smallish dark-haired man, thin faced, clad in a sober grey suit, wearing a pair of head-phones, the free flex of which was slung carelessly over his shoulder.

After a minute of vague half-remembering, the realisation of where he had seen that figure previously struck Rostof like a blow.

He was looking at himself!

After a shock such as Rostof had passed through, and coming up against an impossibility like this, a normal man might be excused for becoming a little deranged mentally. Through his mind there flashed wild conjectures, of which the chief seemed to be that he was either dreaming or mad—or perhaps he was dead. I think myself that only his scientific training saved his reason. For while his brain rocked with bewilderment, it still mechanically observed and noted. An underlying curiosity drove him on, though his conscious mind was still too dazed with shock to function properly.

The figure in grey when he first noticed it, was walking—backwards. It jerked back, like a film run in reverse, towards the door, passed through it; and Rostof followed like a dream-walker. His other self turned sharply to the right into the narrow cupboard of a radio-room, walked—still backwards—to the chair and sat down in it. Then he pushed the phone leads into their sockets and appeared to be listening.

Rostof approached the figure slowly and touched it gingerly on the shoulder, then took hold of it more firmly and shook it—or tried to. For in spite of this strongest efforts he could make not the slightest impression on the sitting figure. It was like touching an image of granite, save that this one undoubtedly lived. Even the cloth of the coat had no resiliency, was as hard and unyielding to the touch as adamant.

He tugged vainly, he spoke, shouted in the man's ear. No response. Rostof studied the face of the man in the chair; it was without a doubt his own face, just as if he were looking into a mirror. With that thought came a wild fear that in some incredible manner he had been transported into some stranger's body in an exchange of personalities. In sudden, unreasoning terror he ran to the small mirror that hung on the wall, dreading to see an unknown face reflected there.

What he saw came with the terrific shock of utter unexpectedness. *There was no reflection at all.*

THE PROBLEM

He could see the opposite wall, part of the room, everything in the normal range of view, but no face looked out at him. It was an uncanny, shaking experience. Crane and stretch as he liked, he could see not a scrap of his own body in the mirror.

He looked down. There was his body, indubitably. He held his hand before his eyes, crooked the fingers; they were there all right, he could swear. He slapped his thigh, felt the sting of his palm, saw the red mark grow on his skin.

In that moment Rostof was like a small child, bewildered by events totally out of its normal experience, scared and lost. Everything in the world seemed to have gone suddenly and horribly wrong, and he wanted badly to find something right and normal which he could use as an anchor for his tottering reason. He wanted to talk with friends, to see human beings acting sanely again.

He ran back into the main laboratory. Schouten and Matheson were at one of the work-benches. He went up to Schouten and spoke to him, tugged at his sleeve, and a thrill of horror shot through him as he realised that the same dreadful, granite-like hardness had taken possession of his friend. He could make no more impression on Schouten than on a moving statue.

He turned quickly to Matheson, and the history-master was in the same condition. Rostof frantically punched him in the ribs, and yelped with pain, for his knuckles were barked and skinned as though he had struck a brick wall. A sickening sense of impotency, of being nothing more substantial than a ghost, swept over him.

As he watched his friends, another thing struck him. All their movements were in reverse. Matheson was filing up an angle and he drew his file *back* across the metal at each stroke, while the forward stroke was made through the air. Queerest of all, Schouten was cutting through a metal strip with a hack-saw, and here again his strokes seemed all wrong; but the amazing thing was that the cut, instead of growing deeper into the metal, *was growing smaller* and shrinking towards the top.

He watched in fascination until at last the saw-blade reached the top and was withdrawn, leaving virgin, untouched metal behind. Suddenly Schouten stepped backward and cannoned into Rostof; but he did not falter or deviate in his stride the least fraction of an inch. It was Rostof who, feeling as if he had been struck by a steam-engine, went staggering aside to sprawl on the floor.

He got up and watched his friend stalk solemnly backward to the tool-rack and hang the hack-saw up. Telling me afterwards, Rostof said:

"I think I went a little crazy then. I stood in the middle of the floor and screamed, shouted at the top of my voice at them. I cursed and raved, pleaded and prayed, waved my arms to heaven. I begged them to quit fooling and be sane, though goodness only knows what joke I could have thought they were playing. I believe that for a bit I blubbered like a kid. . . ."

As I have said before, the inborn scientist in him probably saved his reason. After a while, when he had quietened down, his mind fastened on the problem before him. The problem; that was it! If he could only keep calm and watch and think, perhaps some explanation would offer itself. At least he was still alive (though he was not perfectly sure about that), and he could still reason and use his wits, apparently.

At this juncture Matheson left the bench and walked from the room, again backwards. Rostof followed him into the little kitchen where they had a fire and a wash-bowl and prepared an occasional late meal. Matheson made toward the towel which hung on a roller beside the bowl, turned round, and appeared to be going through the motions of drying his hands. As the other watched, a gurgling sound from the basin attracted his attention.

A flood of soapy, dirty-looking water was welling up from the drain outlet and rapidly filling the basin. Rostof, absorbed in this phenomenon, had barely time to skip aside as Matheson moved to the basin, inserted the plug, took the soap from the dish and proceeded to wash his hands.

When he had finished, Rostof's eyes again widened in surprise, for the water was perfectly clean and clear, while Matheson's hands were grimy, but apparently quite dry; and as he made an adjustment to the tap, the water suddenly began to flow *upwards* in a narrow pillar through the tap.

Rostof let Matheson go back to the lab unattended while he watched this amazing phenomenon of water spurting up through the tap. A miniature water-spout, with a few queer splashed about its base, quivered up straight and true through the orifice; the level in the basin rapidly dropped, and only an inch or so remained in the bottom when Matheson returned. As the last few drops shot up into the tap, he twisted the handle, and there was left only an empty, perfectly dry basin.

Matheson made backwards for the lab door, and Rostof was following when he happened to glance casually at the clock. He noted the time mechanically, and was continuing after the other when a sudden thought froze him in his tracks.

He looked again at the clock. There was no mistake; the hands showed seventeen minutes past six. Yet when he had come out of the radio room and glanced up at the clock in passing, it had been *half*-past six.

BACKWARD IN TIME

He stood as if petrified, gazing at the clock. It was in that moment that the first flicker of the nerve-shaking idea licked through his mind. It was a possible, but crazy explanation of the whole, ridiculous affair. He slumped into a chair and tried to think coherently.

Was it possible that when that puzzling flare of light had come, his Time-sense had in some way been reversed—turned back to front, as it were? Or to put it another way, had he been plunged into a Time Stream which flowed in exactly the opposite direction to the normal one?

You understand, of course, that at that time Rostof had not the vaguest notion of what had happened as he stood by the gap, save a suspicion that some form of electrical discharge had taken place. But the more he thought, the more it seemed possible that only some such incredible reversal of Time could explain the phenomena which so puzzled him.

If he were steadily progressing backward in Time, then the surprising topsy-turviness of external actions became more understandable. His friends walking backward, for instance; the water that flowed upwards; his ability to see himself. He was simply witnessing the Past, like seeing a film run in reverse. But more than witnessing—he was *living* through the Past, every second taking him deeper and deeper into it.

He looked at the clock again. He was already separated from the world of normal Time by three-quarters of an hour. He began to sweat as the horror of the situation took hold of him. Three-quarters of an hour is not long in everyday life, but to him it was as good as eternity. It seemed he was doomed never again to converse with his friends or any human being, never to see again a sane, understandable world.

Try to picture him as he sat there, naked, defenceless, fighting to keep calm and grapple intelligently with a situation that should have sent him mad. Imagine his incredible loneliness; one small human, plunging towards a vague and misty future which lay in the Past, while with each second everything that stood for friendship, safety and comfort, was hurtling farther away in the opposite direction. . . .

Grimly, he dragged his mind from the image and concentrated it on the scientific side of the problem. For a while he could not understand the impenetrable hardness of external objects which he had experienced; it seemed they ought rather to be of intangible transience, much as a dream, since he was re-viewing the Past. But a moment's thought gave him the logical answer.

The Past is definite, shaped, unalterable, as nothing else in Creation is. Therefore, to argue that he could make the slightest impression on it, that he could move or alter an object here was to argue that he could change the whole history of the world or cosmos. Everything he saw about him had happened, and could not be changed in any way. On the other hand, he was fluid, movable, alterable, since *his* future still lay before him, even if it had been reversed; he was the intruder, the anomaly. In any clash between himself and the Past, then, the Past would prove irresistible every time.

No wonder they could not feel him shout; no wonder they could not feel a punch. He was no more than a chimera.

He sat gnawing his lip and frowning at the clock for almost an hour. There would be all sorts of queer effects. He would have to keep dodging out of people's way or run the risk of being brained; if he happened to get into the path of a fly or a bee going at speed, it would bore through him more surely than any bullet. The Sun, for him, would sink in the east and rise in the west. He would see trees and plants growing downward until they shrank into the ground and turned to seed;; the seed would leap through the air or be carried away by birds to the parent tree, would change to flowers, to buds, back through all the endless cycle. . . .

At last he roused himself and made his way to the outer door. Fortunately for him, it was ajar, and he managed to squeeze through; he had no desire to be shut in when Shouten left at three o'clock.

The district where the laboratory was situated was not a busy one, and before long he realised that it would be best for him to avoid all busy thorough fares. Never until now had he realised how much the world depended on forward movement, how rare in normal life is retrogression. It was a startling experience to see motor-cars suddenly whiz round corners, travelling backwards; to see pigeons take off from the ground stern first in a flurry of wings; to see a black feather which had fallen from a crow's wing in the Past float up into the air and neatly fix itself into the bird's sable plumage as it flew solemnly backwards.

He found it almost impossible to pre-judge people's movements; all his instinctive mental calculations were upset. A man looking into a shop window would without warning slip into reverse and come striding at Rostof, who would leap wildly aside; a ball lying in the roadway would suddenly start into life come rolling and bouncing along, then fly past his head into the hand of the urchin who had once thrown it. After a time he learned to keep a wary eye on any movable object near-by, but the process of learning was a painful business and involved many bruises and shakings.

DOOMED . . .

All through Thursday, as the afternoon drew on to morning and the Sun rose to the south and began to arch downward into the east, Rostof wandered at random, his plight almost forgotten in the unparalleled novelty of his surroundings, which appealed to the scientist in him. There seemed no reason to hope that the condition in which he found himself would ever revert to normal, though the prospect of spending the rest of his life as a helpless ghost among the scenes of an iron-bound Past was not pleasant.

But by the middle of the morning, the thought of a prolonged existence in this state ceased to bother him. For he realised what he should have done before, that unless a miracle happened, in a few days he would be dead of starvation and thirst.

Not until the pangs of hunger drove him to try to sample some sandwiches from a coffee-stall was the realisation brought home to him. Tug and strain as he might, he could not lift the smallest crumb. He tried bending his head to bite a piece from a sandwich, but it was like trying to bite a concrete slab. He tried to lift a cup of coffee, but it was immobile as a rock. In a sudden panic he dipped his fingers into the cup, trying to scoop up a little of the liquid. He could not even ripple the surface; it was like scratching at a block of brown glass.

He stood there in dismay. It was only to be expected, of course. In any case, even if he had been able to contrive any crumb of food down his throat he could not have digested it; and if he moved away it would simple rip a hole in him, since it would inevitably stay fixed in its own position.

Strangely enough, the knowledge that he was a doomed man did not utterly unnerve him. In spite of the jokes that were levelled at him, I think there was the stuff of a truly great character in that insignificant little schoolteacher. His Odyssey is a more bizarre one than any Ulysses ever dreamed of, yet the hunger for knowledge, the intellectual interest of a pioneer in a mighty experiment, transcended for him the fear of a slow and lonely death.

He even smiled wryly as a workman stepped backwards up to the stall, turned, picked up an empty cup, lifted it to his lips, and after a moment set down a steaming full cup of coffee. The man made munching motions with is jaws, and presently took from his mouth a morsel of sandwich; more followed, until in a few minutes a complete and untouched ham sandwich lay on the plate before him. Then he took a coin from the proprietor of the stall and put it away in his pocket as he backed briskly away.

Rostof lingered for a second or two longer, fascinated by the sight of steam appearing out of thin air and gushing into the spout of the big coffee-urn, then he, too, went on his way.

When at length the dusk of early morning fell, he began to think of finding somewhere to sleep, but there was to be little sleep for him that night. There was no chance, he soon discovered, of finding anything soft on which to lie. A heap of hay in a stable-yard tempted him, but it was like lying on sharp, hair-thin wire without the slightest yield to it.

For the greater part of the Wednesday night he wandered disconsolately through the empty streets, until fatigue forced him to sit on a door-step and rest his back against the door. If it was hard, it was at least smooth. He dared not let himself sleep for fear he should be sleeping when anyone came in or out of the door, but towards Wednesday evening he dropped into a troubled sleep for an hour.

With the chiming of ten o'clock from the church tower he awoke, and rose wearily to move on. The Wednesday night crowds were still about, and he felt it would not be safe to sleep longer. He rubbed a hand over his stubbled chin as he went.

You will note that the metabolism of his body still continued normally. His hair still grew, his body became fatigued and needed food, blood circulated steadily in his veins, his heart thumped in regulation time. Which explains why he was able to remember the whole train of events from Tuesday to Thursday, and back again to Tuesday; as far as his physical self was concerned it was one unbroken period of time.

Throughout the Wednesday he worked more and more out towards the countryside, avoiding the busier thoroughfares. He was feeling faint with hunger and exhaustion and his reflexes were slower in responding to danger signals, as was proved by one or two narrow escapes.

Once he came upon a cat walking gravely backward towards a low wall, and unthinkingly tried to cut in between cat and wall. As he drew level, however, the cat crouched and suddenly sprang tail first through the air towards the top of the wall. Rostof was not quite quick enough in dodging, and she caught him a glancing blow on the shoulder that sent him spinning a dozen yards and left a raw gash that dripped blood along his arm. After that he roused himself to walk more warily; but despite his care, he was almost caught in the morning.

WAITING FOR DEATH

The Wednesday morning was dull, with low grey clouds overhead. About eleven o'clock, he noticed a curious dampness which spread in patches over the roads. As time passed this dampness ran together and increased, until by nine o'clock something like a thin sheet of ice or glass covered the paths, and brown water was gushing up from the drains and culverts.

Rostof was surprisingly slow to grasp the meaning of this, until he saw something like a streak of silver shoot up from the road, and another odd one here and there; then the explanation and the thrill of imminent danger shot through his mind, and he leaped for a providential near-by passageway.

Inside five minutes he was gazing out at the strangest rain shower he had ever seen, a shower in which the drops, like deadly silver bullets, shot up at lightning speed from the ground and vanished into the sky. Pools in the road split up into a myriad tiny streams that spread away in all directions and finally dissipated themselves in drops which hurled themselves at the clouds above. Had he been caught out in that queer rainstorm his body would have been slashed to ribbons in a matter of seconds.

After about twenty minutes the shower abated, and presently he could see dry patches between the spots. Then the dry patches joined up and became bigger, while the spots of rain became fewer, until at length the last one had flashed upward out of sight and a bone-dry road was left behind.

Rostof was hampered a good deal in the outlying roads and lanes by grass borders which kept him to the roadway. Where the grass was clipped close it was possible to walk on it, even though it felt like treading on close packed nails; but where it grew long it would have lacerated his feet like thin slivers of glass.

As Tuesday night drew on, therefore, he was undecided whether to return to the town to find an unfrequented corner to sleep in, or whether to push on farther in the hope of finding a farm. But, seeing a large house standing among trees in its own grounds, he decided to try there, for he was feeling wretchedly weary.

He turned up the winding drive and hunted about for a smooth spot in which to lie down. Passing an open window, a weird cacophony of noise startled him, and he could not think what it was until, looking through the window, he saw a gramophone on the table. It was the first time he had heard a tune played backwards, and try as he might he could not place the melody.

Sounds, of course, were still audible to him, but like all other things they were heard in reverse, and were often totally unrecognisable. Speech came from the lips of the people about him as mere gibberish, while the song of birds was changed to disjointed notes; even the hooting of cars was different. Only sounds without change of note, such as an engine whistle or the clatter of horses' hooves, seemed familiar.

He spent the night lying on the top of a flat porch over the main entrance of the house though sleep did not come until the Tuesday evening. He ached in every bone and the roof-top seemed terribly hard, though fortunately he was not cold. Throughout his experiences he felt no change of temperature.

He awoke when the Sun was already climbing back into the sky, and lay for a long time reluctant to move. For the first time, utter hopelessness swept over him in a dark flood. He had not eaten for two days and nights, his shoulder was stiff and throbbed unceasingly. He had had nothing with which to staunch the flow of blood from the gash, and loss of blood coupled with hunger and fatigue made him feel sickly and faint.

There seemed no point in rousing himself to continue his wandering, for sooner or later death would come and bring surcease from the dull gnawing of pain. He wondered vaguely if in death his body would revert to a normal state, or whether it would still be borne on into the vast mausoleum of the Past. . . ?

In the late afternoon he clambered stiffly and slowly down from the porch, and for a time wandered around the house. At the back kitchen door was open, and the sight of a plate of newly-baked cakes on the table drove him to try to abstract one. It was useless, of course, and after skinning his knuckles in an endeavour to make an impression on them, he went outside again to avoid the sight of them.

He made his way round to the front of the house with the intention of taking to the road again, and was skirting the main lawn when something attracted his attention. A small brown bird was flying backwards across the lawn, about five feet from the ground; but it was not this which seemed so strange. It was the fact that the bird was flying far more slowly than any natural bird ever does.

Previously, all movements about him, although in reverse, had been invariably at normal speeds. But this bird was like something in a slow-motion film; it was simply drifting backward, and he could count each wing-beat. He watched it with interest, and when it was almost in the centre of the lawn his eyes widened in surprise. For it had stopped in mid-air!

In a moment he was across to it. There, five feet above the ground, the small brown bird hung as if suspended by invisible wires, frozen into an exquisitely carved, tiny statue. He passed his hand all around it, below and above, and finally took hold of it. It was brittle hard and utterly immovable, exactly as all other objects were in this alien Time Stream.

BACK TO NORMAL

He suddenly realised, with a faint thrill of fear, that the whole world seemed to have become noticeably silent. A vast quiet was all about him; not the faintest twitter of a bird, not a rustle of a branch, not a click or tap sounded anywhere. He stood stock-still as if afraid to stir lest some other nightmare was about to beset him.

As he slowly turned his head, he discovered that all motion, too, seemed to have ceased. A gardener who had been bent over a border was grotesquely crouched, one hand half-stretched out. The slight dip and sway of the branches in the breeze had stopped, a film of smoke from a chimney balanced in the air like a spray of blue glass. The whole Earth seemed to be holding its breath.

Then a second of unutterable tension tugged at his body and a shock of reeling nausea struck him. His body seemed to be riven into a million pieces, yet he could not stir of cry. There was a brief flash of all-enveloping darkness. Then the tension snapped like a released rubber band, and he was staggering slightly, wild-eyed.

The small brown bird was flashing off toward the bushes—flying *forwards!* The gardener stood gazing at him with a ludicrous look of amazement on his face. Rostof realised, with a sudden wild thrill of hope, that the man could *see* him. He ran forward, babbling incoherently.

The next instant he was shaking the hand of the astounded Mr. Curle, laughing and weeping at the same time. . . .

Well, there you have Rostof's own story, and the main facts of the case. But there are one or two more facts which you can call evidence or coincidence, whichever way your inclinations lean.

Rostof said that on the Wednesday night he had been attracted by the crowd to the Elite cinema at Highgate. He was on the outskirts of the crowd, and did not have a very good view; but he at least saw the firemen break in by the second floor balcony, and the clouds of dense black smoke which rolled away on the night breeze. His story appeared in the Wednesday morning papers, and that same evening at six o'clock the Elite caught fire and the fire brigade was called out.

Rostof, of course, wasn't there. He was in hospital, sleeping peacefully. But it is a coincidence that he should have guessed—or dreamed—that a fire would occur on that identical night.

Again, what can you make of this? Schouten and Matheson went to visit Rostof in hospital, naturally. They were carrying on with the experimental routine at the laboratory, and let him know how the work was progressing. On Thursday evening, they were both working in the main room when a freak thunderstorm came up from the south; unusual for the time of year, but not unprecedented.

There were one or two desultory flashes of lightning, then at 6.31 p.m. precisely a vivid flash struck the roof and passed by the giant copper discharge gap to earth. The gap had been partly charged, and was due for breakdown at seven o'clock. The upper cone was badly melted, the ground plate buckled and fused, and much of the adjacent apparatus was fused or burnt.

Unaccountably, immediately after the flash they found a complete suit of grey cloth, underwear, boots and socks, badly singed and burnt, beside the gap, together with a twisted object which at first was unrecognisable. Later, however, they judged it to be the remains of a pair of headphones, though how either they or the suit got there was more than the two men could say.

In my own mind I feel convinced that Rostof actually went on from Tuesday to Thursday in the first place, conducting his classes and behaving in every way as a normal person should. Then, on that Thursday evening, he was twisted into a reversed Time Stream and started to come back on his own tracks, as it were. Thus, he would see himself in his former existence, a helpless spectator of his own past.

But when the process slowed down and stopped, and he was released into the normal Time Stream on Tuesday at 3 p.m., an apparent anomaly appears at once. There would be two Rostofs existing at the same time! Would have been, that is, except for the inflexible law which states that a man cannot exist in two separate places during the same period of time.

But the instant that he came back into the normal Time Stream, and appeared on Mrs. Van der Rorvik's lawn, his former Tuesday-to-Thursday existence was automatically cancelled, obliterated, washed out as if it had never been. Which explains his startling disappearance from the Grammar School. He had to start the Tuesday-to-Thursday Time journey anew— but this time in a hospital ward. Yet since his metabolism and physical processes were unchanged throughout the adventure, he could still *remember* his former existence, even if it no longer existed in the minds of other people.

Of the mechanism of his transition I can say little, since, as I remarked before, I am no physicist. It seems possible that the lightning flash struck him, or the main force was diverted through the headphones, with the result that Rostof was twisted out of the normal Time Stream. Whether the presence of the discharge gap had any effect or not, it is hard to say; certainly, the freakish effects of lightning have long proved difficult to explain.

It is a curious case, but I am inclined to think it is not unique. In the past there have been many unexplained disappearances; there are also several authenticated instances of naked men who have suddenly appeared, apparently from nowhere, and been unable to give a coherent account of where they came from or who they were.

Anyway, you have heard Rostof's story, and may form your own opinion as to the most probable explanation of the whole strange affair. Though you may be inclined to ask: what does Rostof himself think about it all?

I can only tell you this. Nicolai Rostof has changed his name to Norman Robinson, has grown a moustache and wears horn-rimmed spectacles. He has gone to work in a certain industrial town whose name I have promised not to reveal, and where he is not known. Rostof is trying to forget.

The Time-Drug

If you are a layman you have probably never heard of my friend, Stadtland, for he was a scientist, and no very famous one at that . . . and yet, if the truth were known, he should be acclaimed as one of the greatest who ever lived. But it is possible that you may have read of the repercussions of his last and greatest experiment, of his shadow self, and of the inexplicable occurrence which caused a ripple of excitement and mystery in a tiny Lincolnshire market town; although it never appeared under any of these headings.

If you care to probe your subconscious memory, you may stir up vague recollections of "The Chyne Apparition" which, a year or so back, caused the old hash of ghost stories to ferment and bubble again in the Press. *The Times*, even, had a few paragraphs about the Chyne Phenomena. The Psychical Research Society showed more interest than anyone; but the public never reads their reports, and in any case, they could make little of it.

People made a few desultory guesses, and everyone was wrong. I could have made a reasonable shot at the truth, and heard myself called a liar for my pains. But Stat *was* a great scientist—a genius; and I am setting down here what I know in an effort to pay the only tribute to him that will ever appear. If you don't believe it, well—you needn't. The fact remains that he was my friend.

Stat was a real professor, even if a poor one—Professor Mihailoff Stadtland, to give him his full designation. As his name suggests, he was half Russian, but I don't think he ever spent more than a few months in Russia. To see him, you would imagine he was one of these Bohemian writers or artists you read about, for he was eternally untidy, and his mop of lank, black hair stuck out at all angles.

His untidiness was emphasized by his thinness and leanness; he seemed all bones and awkwardness. He had drifted through a few heterogeneous jobs at one time or another—chemical expert for a technical journal, jobbing tutor, druggist's assistant, and wages clerk—until finally he bought an old army hut a mile outside the small town of Chyne, and settled down to scrape along on a small income from his savings and the occasional windfall that came of having a scientific paper published.

The greater part of the hut was converted into a laboratory, with a dash of studio and carpenter's den about it, and he spent most of his time in it; turned out some good results too. His paper on "Extra-Sensory Perception" created a minor stir, and he was a pioneer in the effects of various drugs on telepathic abilities at the time when Estabrooks and Brugmann were starting their mass experiments on college students.

I would drop in on him at odd intervals and share expenses, while I hunted round for a fresh place to make for. Sometimes I was flush, and we lived well; at others I was glad of the bread and cheese and onions, and the watery cocoa, we had for summer. Stat was always glad to see me, though, as I was to see his lean face crack in a grin; and the old shack was perhaps the nearest thing to home I have known.

One autumn—my job of the moment was radio operator—I signed off a timber-carrier at Hull, and decided to run down to Chyne and take a week of two's vacation, then maybe get a shore job for the winter, if I was lucky. I was sick of the sea, the stink of oil and the thump of engines, and I wanted to walk in beech woods and see blue wood-smoke rising in an autumn sky once again.

Stat gave me a welcome that made me realise what a real homecoming can be, and started to get a hot supper ready straight away, for it was pretty late when I arrived. I dumped my gear in my old room and tried to help until, in desperation, he made be sit in the battered wicker chair by the fire, out of the way.

"Well, how are things with you, old chap?" I asked, as I fished out my pipe.

"Fine, Frank! Very fine." He straightened up from the frying- pan and stabbed a fork in the air for emphasis, his blue eyes a more vivid blue than ever.

"At last I'm on to a really big things; one of those things that are stumbled on be accident once every few centuries. I only just completed the final experiments and got practical results the day before yesterday, and even now there's a lot I don't know. Oh, a vast lot! It's really a totally new field of science that this will open up."

A suspicious smell of burning rose in the air, and he made a dive for the pan, adding, "I'll try to explain after you've had some grub."

And when we had reached the stage of coffee and cheese, and a sense of mellow well-being, having completed the first interchange of reminiscence, he did.

"You will remember," he said seriously, "how years ago, I was hunting on the trail of that philosopher's stone of science, time-travel?

You used to rag me about chasing that myth; a wild-goose chase after a meaningless phrase which H.G. Wells brought into existence. I half-believed it would prove fruitless, myself, but the subject fascinated me, and I pursued it as an intellectual exercise, if nothing else.

"I was handicapped in one respect by the lack of vast reservoirs of power, but I satisfied myself that, theoretically at least, sheer power would be useless. You can't catapult a man forward in time with the sling of a few million volts, or by smashing his atoms with gamma rays.

"I read everything there was on the subject; followed Dunne in treating time as a regress, and treated it as a dimension. Maeterlinck, in a little book, *The Life of Space*, had some very acute observations to make on the fourth dimension, that made me think I was on the right track for a while. But I failed."

He sighed. "I spent for years at it, and got nothing but some obscure knowledge and the realisation that, if I were to solve the problem, I should need two or three fortunes and an extra lifetime. And then—you know, it's happened before, Frank—in pursuing a totally different line of research, I stumbled by sheer fool's luck on at least half the answer. *I can explore the Past.*"

I knew enough of Stat to take him seriously. "You mean literally—physically?"

He smiled. "Not physically, Frank, but mentally. I can see and hear everything that has happened, back to the Stone Age, back to a mist-and-thunder-shrouded beginning of the Earth, past that to when the Sun was a planetless star, and beyond. . . .

"This was the way of it," he went on earnestly. "I became interested in the problem of sleep, as other, better men have done before me. At first, I was only interested in the causes and need of it; and Durham, in 1860, noted that whatever decreases the cerebral circulation, and at the same time is not inconsistent with the general health of the body, tends to induce and assist sleep. I started from this point and worked forward, getting one or two minor, but new facts. Then one day, I was struck by a radically fresh aspect of the investigation.

"If we go to sleep, or if we are drugged, unconscious, we lose all sense of the passage of time. To our awareness, it is as though we have leaped so many hours into the futures, without any interim. True, our bodies remain there, and are changing metabolically while we sleep, but to all intents, mentally, we have skipped a few hours into the future. There are one or two cases where people have been sleeping for years; if one of these persons should wake, it must seem to him as if he has been whisked into the future by magical means. Remember *The Sleeper Awakes* . . . ?" I nodded, dazedly.

"If we can mentally leap forward in time, why can't we reverse the process and probe backward mentally? Every natural process should be capable of being reversed, if we can only tap the secret.

"Then what would seem to be the exact opposite of sleep? At first you say, naturally, the state of waking. But is it? Suppose wakefulness is simply a middle or neutral state, sleep is at one extreme of the scale, and at the other end of the scale is the true antithesis of sleep that we have only remotely approached and never experienced.

"In sleep, the faculties and mental life are slowed down to practically a standstill. Theoretically, then, to reverse the process we should increase the speed of mental living and thinking, somewhat in the manner in which Wells's *Accelerator* was suppose to act. This is borne out in practice by the fact that an increase in the cerebral circulation induces wakefulness.

"Now, suppose we intensify a hundredfold, a thousandfold, the rate of mental living; far past the normal working state you experience in conscious life. In that case, time, instead of being speeded up to the point of leaping a space, *would be slowed down*. Other people's movements would become incredibly slow and snail-like. At the point where the movement of time reached zero, there would be no change or motion visible at all; not the slightest. Time would be non-existent!"

Stat fairly wriggled in his seat with the intensity of his purpose, and pointing a lean forefinger, said slowly:

"And now if we still more increase the speed of mental action, *beyond* this point. What happens?

I had followed his argument easily enough up to now, and it impressed me. I thought for a moment or two, then replied:

"Why, one would think that logically . . . yes; time would begin to take a backward drift. If you reduce an action to zero, but still keep the reducing force exerted and increased, then the action must commence in complete reversal."

"Exactly!" snapped Stat. "We should see movements around us gathering speed once more, but acting always in a reverse direction. We should see the past unrolling itself to the very beginning of Time. . . . I have journeyed into the past myself!"

He leaned back in his chair, and continued:

"The tremendous difficulty was to find the right process that would increase the cerebral circulation sufficiently—and safely. I thought at first of trying some means of electrical stimulus, but found it useless and dangerous. Then my old training in drugs came to my aid. You will recall some of my experiments with the effects of drugs on the telepathic ability?

"In three months I arrived, by means of elimination, at two which seemed to offer promise. One was the *anhalonium* alkaloid group; Heffter investigated seven different bases, derived from the various species of cactus, and noted that certain of them possessed the peculiar property of vastly increasing the vividness of sensory impressions. The other was a powder of the root of *piper methysticum,* a Pacific Islands plant known as *ava,* or *kava-kava,* among the natives; it is used as an intoxicant, and sometimes as a drug, on the Continent.

"Eventually, I produced a solution in which *anhalonine* and *ava* formed the chief constituents, together with a small proportion of other drugs. It was a mental stimulant such as has never existed since, perhaps, the days of ancient Eastern science, and had the advantage of producing little or no reaction. Its effect was a substantial confirmation of my theory, for while the body was rendered practically helpless, mental perception was speeded up to a point where external motions were almost non-existent.

"But it was not efficient enough to produce the backward time-drift I had hoped for. That I did not achieve for another six months, and I had almost begun to despair of reaching a solution, when I found that high-frequency electo-magnetic waves passed through the brain cells enormously increased the effect of the drug. Some mice and a dog, on whom I tried the process, passed into a state resembling catalepsy, but came out of it when the radiations were switched off, quite fit and unharmed.

"The day before yesterday, I took an injection of the drug, and immediately switched on the short-wave radiations, which were due to be cut off by an automatic device at the end of three minutes. Frank, it worked perfectly!"

Stat pushed back his chair. "Come into the lab, and take a look at the whole arrangement while I tell you of my first trip."

The laboratory, as I have mentioned, was apt to be a bit chaotic, but as my friend switched on the light, I saw that half the room had been cleared of all apparatus and oddments save for a solidly built, high-backed arm-chair standing beside a small card-table. Attached to an upright of the chair, so as to be on a level with an occupant's head, was a tiny, parabolic frame-aerial; and I noticed wires leading from this to a large, black container beneath the seat of the chair. On the right-hand arm-rest was a switch and a dial.

Stat went across to a small cupboard, unlocked it, and took out a small vial of a dark brown liquid which, when he held it up to the light, appeared to turn faintly purplish.

"This," he said, "is the Time-Drug, the most marvelous potion of any yet concocted—the key to that baffling door of the Past. This chair is where I sit when taking the drug; an injection is the most efficient means of employing it, and immediately afterwards I drop the syringe on the table, and switch on the short-wave oscillator you see there beneath the chair. Its range, of course, is extremely short; but the high-frequency radiations pass through the sitter's brain cells, and complete the liberating process.

"The automatic control on the arm shuts off the oscillator at any set interval, and allows the mental processes to return to normal, though this requires a slight effort of will on the part of the subject. I have not found any time limit when the properties of the Time-Drug show signs of weakening. . . .

"My first experience of the drug was rather terrifying, as the sensation was utterly alien, and I had no sure knowledge of what would happen. The first impressions were that of swift-growing physical weakness, which changed to a total lack of bodily feeling and a moment of darkness; the power of a mental imagery and impression is vastly increased, which appears to make the transition period longer than it can actually be.

"The sense of sight is lost, but you find that you are fully aware of all that is taking place about you, even down to shades of colour, and movements taking place behind or above the normal field of vision. A sixth sense comes into operation, or perhaps the ordinary capacity for gathering impressions from the external world is intensified a thousand-fold. At any rate, the effect is like that of a vivid dream, in which one is conscious of everything except possessing a body.

"I found that, if no volition was exercised, the reversed time-drift was in only a slightly greater ratio than the normal time-flow; that is, an hour of reversed time seemed equivalent to about eighty minutes of normal time. *But,* by exercising my will, I could leap backward in time at inconceivably greater rates.

"At first, I explored backward only for a few days, and found that sufficiently interesting to have spent all the time at my disposal on it. To watch one's-self performing tasks many hours old is a decidedly novel experience, to say the least!"

I had been looking over the Time-Chair while he talked, and found the electrical lay-out simple and understandable enough; any radio man could have fixed up the short-wave transmitter. Probably a chemist would have found the analysis of the Time-Drug just as simple; but it was the combination of the two which released this new and uncanny energy, and the more I thought about it, the more impressed I became. Its very simplicity made it seem credible, and I respected Stadtland's intelligence enough to know that he meant every word of what he had been saying.

"You'll let me try the drug, won't you, Stat?" I asked. "You know that poking my nose into the out-of-the-ordinary and bizarre has always been my weakness, and this is one of the weirdest things under the Sun. How about an experiment tonight?"

Stat hesitated. "No, Frank; if you don't mind, I'd rather not. It's late, and you'll be tired. But I'd like you to stop and help me with the experiments for a week or two, if you can; there's a heap of work to be done yet, and a lot more I want to know about the process. To-morrow morning we'll start, and you shall have your trip into the past."

With that I had to be content, but I slept little that night. The more I thought of seeing into the past, the more interesting the possibilities became. I wondered if historians would offer Stat a fortune for his invention, and dreamed that I was writing a letter to Sir Flinders Petrie to tell him that the Great Pyramid had really been built by Harald Blacktooth.

Next morning, however, Stat was up long before I was awake, and roused me out to breakfast. After the meal was cleared away, we went into the laboratory.

"First of all, Frank," said Stat, "I'll take a short trip so that you can see the procedure." On the small card-table by the chair were a case of hypodermic needles, two test-tubes of the Time-Drug, notebooks and pencils, and a clock. Stat seated himself in the chair, and adjusted the setting of the control on the chair-arm. "I've set it for a sixty-second period of transmission, which will be ample for this purpose."

He took a clean needle, filled it from one of the test-tubes, and carefully replaced the tube in the rack. Next, he injected the drug into his left fore-arm, quickly placed the needle on the table, leaned back in the chair, and snapped over the switch on the arm-rest.

There came the low hum of a small motor-generator from the transmitter, and with the sound Stat seemed to slacken and become still. I watched closely, but could detect only the faintest signs of breathing; his eyes stared straight ahead, without life or interest.

Only the steady hum of the motor broke the silence in the lab. I watched the second-hand on the clock anxiously as it jerked its way over sixty seconds, and thought I had never known them to last so long. But, dead on the end of the minute, there was the click of a relay, and the song of the motor died into silence. A second or two afterwards, Stat stirred, and smiled into my anxious face.

"All O.K., Frank! Now, if you want your trip, go ahead."

I sat in the chair, exactly as Stat had done, while he stood by and set the automatic relay.

"I'm giving you ten minutes," he said, "which will be enough for a first trip. You can have longer later on, when you've got the knack of time-traveling. Bear in mind that you have only to will yourself to be at a certain date, and you get there; but keep a calm hold on your thoughts, or it will seem a bit chaotic."

I filled the needle, and pricked it into my fore-arm, then dropped it on the table and closed the switch. I felt more than a little nervous excitement as I leaned back; almost I expected to feel the high-frequency radiations pulsing through my brain. But it was nothing like that, of course.

The first sensations were very like those produced by taking gas at the dentist's. A sense of overwhelming inertia and lassitude; a darkness that welled up out of every corner and dimmed the sight; a buzzing in the ears. The darkness leaped into oblivion; all bodily feeling vanished; I floated for an instant that seemed at the same time eternity. Yet I had not lost consciousness—rather, my mind seemed charged with power, vital and living as it had never been before in my life.

Slowly, as if I could see and my eyes were becoming accustomed to a dim light, I became aware of scenes growing all around me. It was still the laboratory, and I was seeing it as if in a dream, as though I were a bodiless entity who could see the whole at once. It was not really sight, for my eyes were useless—dead—back in the shell I had left in the Time-Chair. It was an *awareness*, which sensed colours and sounds with a clarity that human eyes and ears could never possess.

I saw Stat, and he appeared to be talking to someone—why, to myself! It as a shock to see myself standing there; like being dead and reviewing one's past life. Perhaps death may be simply this, a release in Time. . . . The actions of Stat were queer, however, in a way I could not understand, until I saw him step backwards and sit in the Time-Chair. Then I knew that time was drifting backward for me, and I was witnessing the past!

I wondered if I could control the process, and thought of being a hundred years back, in 1838. The result was startling. The scene in the lab leaped into chaos; a flickering succession of black and white blurs ensued; then a greyish blur, shot with green and white. In a second or two, the scene steadied, but now the old army hut was gone, and green fields and hedgerows were all about. It seemed autumn again, for a few brown leaves carpeted the grass.

About twenty yards away to the right, a man was plashing a hedge with a long hedge-knife. He wore side-whiskers, and curious, old-fashioned clothes; a round hat like a billy-cock, but with a wavy brim, and long breeches that tucked into the tops of his stockings. A long-stemmed clay pipe was stuck in his mouth.

I watched him for a moment; noticed that his movements, too, were in reverse, and tried to obtain the normal rate of time-flow. At first, I only succeeded in freezing the picture into immobility, or overshooting the mark altogether, so that he vanished. But presently I managed to achieve a slight, constant mental concentration which just counter-acted the backward drift of time, so as to give the illusion of a normal time flow.

I might have been scared had it not all been so fascinating; but when I had gained a rough control over the time-flow, the sense of power and pulsing vitality in my mind utterly banished any trace of fear. It is almost impossible to describe the feeling of exultation and mastery that comes of having the past at one's will; to scan and rescan, look here, look there, as you desire.

I willed myself to drift farther back into the past, and there was the same kaleidoscope of drab hues; it may have been anything from a hundred to five hundred years—I had no set date in mind. But when I mentally called a halt, the scene was almost exactly the same as before, save that now rain was streaming from leaden skies and no human being was in sight. I tried again at odd intervals, but still saw no one; the explanation was probably that the site of the laboratory, years ago, was a spot remote from any habitation.

Then I took a longer swing. Now, the countryside had changed in character. A grove of pine-trees grew nearby, with a rough track—not much more than a cart-track—winding past them. The hedges had disappeared, and the land took on the wilder appearance of a moor, covered with tussocky grass and occasional furze-bushes.

As I watched, there appeared down a bend of the road three figures, curiously clad. At first, I could detect little except the dull gleam of metal, and the waving of some kind of dark plume at their heads. But as they drew nearer, I saw enough to convince me that I was looking at three Roman legionaries, of a time when the timber wolf still hunted in northern Britain.

All were clad alike in close-fitting tunics of scaled metal, with leather about the shoulders; short kilt-like garments with metal along the thighs, sandals, and an arrangement like a shin-guard. They carried small shields on their left fore-arms, and short-bladed swords swung in scabbards at their hips. One had taken off his helmet, with its nodding horse-hair plume, and his crisp, cark curls were ruffled by the wind. He looked young; barely twenty or so.

They were talking and laughing among themselves, and stopped once while one of them scratched a diagram of some sort in the soil with his sword-point to illustrate some fact or other. As they went out of sight behind the pines I tried to follow them but in vain; no slightest special movement seemed possible in the Time Stream.

The three legionaries had so interested me that I returned to the commencing-point and watched the whole scene over again. They had barely turned the corner of the pines, out of sight, when there came a slight but perceptible dimming of the scene and, at the same time, a curious mental tugging at my mind, as if I were tugging at my mind, as if I were being pulled forward in time. It struck me that my ten minutes must be through, and with the thought came the swift blur of passing decades.

Slowly, I found sight coming back to me through my earthly eyes, and I stirred to the feel of a physical body once more. Stat was smiling down at me.

"Well, Frank, how do you like it? Are you felling O.K.?"

I got out of the Time-Chair, and stamped my feet at the solid feel of the floor.

"It's marvelous, Stat! You've found something that beats cinemas and television hollow. There are heaps of mysteries of the past that can be cleared up now—lost knowledge recovered. . . . Why, you can solve the mystery of the Earth's origin, if you want to."

"I know, and I'm selfish enough to want to keep it to myself for a while, before making the process public—it's so tempting to a scientist! In any case, I'm a bit uncertain as to the best means of disposing the discovery. I suppose it's possible to take out a patent on it; or perhaps it ought to be put into the care of a committee of scientists. But I want to get a lot more data first. . . . "

During the days that followed, we worked on clarifying and systematizing our knowledge of the various effects of the process. Because of my lack of scientific knowledge, I took on the part of amanuensis. The drug's formula, directions for its use, and notes on the Time-Chair, were all entered in a large, leather-bound book, together with records of each "expedition" into the past, time ratios, the various effects noted, and so on.

Stat was anxious to ascertain whether continued use of the drug was likely to breed a craving, or have any deleterious effect on the system, and he also kept careful check on the health of us both; but there was no appearance of any such drawback as we progressed in our researches.

I usually made at least one journey into the realms of the Past each day, and of longer duration than my first. My second trip I remember vividly. When my mental release was completed, I concentrated on plunging backward at utmost speed, resolved to penetrate farther than on my first journey. The passage of the years—nay, centuries—showed now, not as a flicker, but as a monotonous, twilight hue, in which not the slightest detail could be distinguished.

When I called a halt, it was an utterly alien scene which appeared around me. I seemed to be about fifteen feet above a sandy clearing, while all about grew a tangle of ferns, some reaching far above my level; low, bulbous-trunked trees, and great rushes and plants whose species I could not even guess at. Vines and creepers made a worse confusion in the tangle, and here and there a dead log projected itself from the sand.

A great reptile, that must have been all of thirty feet high, with a deer-like head and tiny fore-paws, balanced on powerful hind legs and a thick tail as it browsed on some of the foliage. The Sun shone brightly, but the air seemed slightly steamy, though this may have arisen from the marshy character of the land. A dragon-fly, fully four feet in length and a glory of scintillating electric blue and flashing, gauzy wings, flew across the clearing and away over the tree-tops.

I sensed a slight movement among the mass of foliage, and as I looked a hideous head, a grotesque and monstrous caricature of a frog's, but with great, re-curving yellow teeth, appeared among a group of tree-ferns. The newcomer caught sight of the first creature and bounded into the clearing; if the other were large, this was even larger, and its savage snarl and horrible vitality indicated a carnivore. It may have been a tyrannosaurus, though I am not sure.

The deer-headed reptile saw the oncoming monster and plunged away into the swamp, with the other crashing after it though the rank growths, in hot pursuit. I felt thankful that I had not been present in the clearing in the flesh, for chance of escape from that bounding machine of destruction was small indeed.

One day, when we were looking through our slowly-accumulating mass of data, I mentioned the inability to change one's position in space when "time-traveling".

"Yes," answered Stat; "I've noticed that, and in fact, it was only to be expected. All we do is to send the mind back in time, but there is still a fragile connection with the physical self left in the Chair. If that thread were snapped, anything might happen; but it's safe to say it would be nothing pleasant. You can get over the difficulty by moving the Time-Chair, of course. The released mind simply follows exactly the position of the owner's body.

"There are other interesting facts which have come to light, though. I said once that the process did not involve physical time-travel; but, actually, I believe part—if not all—of the brain is released, and drifts backward in time. The speed of working of the brain cells is increased enormously, so that they must cease to exist in the present. Perhaps not the whole are removed but certainly those cells ensuring mental perception and imagery.

"Again, to a certain extent, the speed of travel in the past and his clearness of vision depend on the will-power and concentration of the traveler," Stat went on. "But I have noted that in extremely long journeys—say, beyond the five-hundred-million-year mark—there is a lag, or hesitancy, in the speed of the return; in fact, it is impossible to return at the speeds one can attain in more recent times. I particularly noticed this on my longest trip, far past the time when the Sun was a planetless star.

"The danger of this lies in the fact that, beyond a certain point—incredibly remote, it is true—it may be impossible to return. Or, again, in exploring towards the beginning of the universe, one may reach a point of self-annihilation, where the universe first explodes into being and commences to expand. The beginning of Time, if you care to call it that. . . .

"There is a great deal about the remoter reaches of the past that I do not understand, as yet, though I know that it will be a risky job to explore them."

Those last words of Stadtland's were to strike me, later, with a new and terrible significance.

We had completed almost a fortnight's work, when there arrived for me a letter from the radio company with whom I had been employed. At that time, there was a serious shortage of wireless operators, and an expanding air force and a boom in shipping had swallowed up what few there were. Consequently, the marine radio companies were hard put to supply even the big cargo vessels and liners.

This was a case in point: a Silver Line vessel was due to sail for the Canaries next day, and her second operator was a hospital case; another could not be found at short notice. Would I oblige by making the trip?

I did not care about going, but three things decided me. Firstly, the depot manager was a decent fellow who had found me a job once when I was flat; secondly, the money would be useful, since I had to live somehow, despite scientific enthusiasm; thirdly, Stat said he would be able to manage by himself, and would probably have the whole process ready for publication by the time I got back. So, in the end, I packed my suitcase and caught the night train.

The voyage is of no interest to the reader, except that it took longer than I expected, for I had to trans-ship at Santa Cruz. In all, it was nearly a month before we docked at East Ham, and I went to the depot to sign off and draw my cheque. With all odds and ends cleared up, and reports and log turned in, I lost no time in making for the station and sending a wire off to let Stat know I was following it fast.

Arriving at Chyne Station, I struck off through the side lanes towards the bungalow, and as I had to pass the "Flying Ship" inn, I thought I would drop in for a drink and say "hello" to old Jim Burdett, who was by way of being a friend of mine. Jim was pleased to see me, and leaned on the bar, willing enough to chat.

"Been away at sea, again sir?"

"Just for one trip," I replied. Down to the Canaries. Nice trip this time of year; plenty of sunshine and fine weather. But I only signed up for the single trip, because I've a fancy for the English countryside in the autumn, and I'm hoping to help Mr. Stadtland with some work he's on."

Jim gave a slight start, and shot a curious glance at me. Then he said slowly: "Mr. Stadtland was a great friend of yours, wasn't he?"

I took a long pull at the beer. "He is," I replied briefly.

Again the old chap gave me an uneasy look, and his hesitation was obvious. At length he said: "Why, maybe with you being away on shipboard, like . . . perhaps you didn't hear of Mr. Stadtland's . . . accident?"

I set the glass down with a thump. Something in the graveness of his tone started a sudden sinking sensation in the pit of my stomach.

"What's that?" No; I've heard nothing. What's happened? He's not hurt, is he?"

Jim's face was troubled. "Why, sir, I'm real sorry . . . real sorry. It's some bad news, like, for you to come home to, and you such pals with him, too. I'd clean forgotten as how it happened after you'd left, and you wouldn't get the local news. Well, it was this way.

"A few days—it couldn't have been a week—after you left, there was a fire up at his bungalow one night. Young Arthur Simmonds was coming down from the farm for a drink when he saw the glow in the sky; he pelted here as hard as he could, and I 'phoned for the town fire brigade. Then me and Joe Briggs and Arthur, we ran like hell up to the hut.

"Joe and Arthur was there first, they bein' younger than me; but there was no sign of Mr. Stadtland, and the place was roaring like a furnace, so they smashed a way in through the work-room window. They found him sitting in a big arm-chair, quite peaceful-like, with his eyes staring open. They lugged him out quick, but though the flames hadn't touched him and there wasn't a mark on him, there didn't seem to be no life in the body.

"We did all we could, and Joe, who's a first-aid man, tried artificial respiration, but it was no use. Joe reckoned as how he must have been suffocated by the fumes, but Doctor Robbs, who came with the brigade, said it was heart failure. He must have gone off in a minute, while he'd been sitting in that big chair—thinking out some of his experiments, maybe. . . .

"He was buried in St. Mary's church-yard, just down the road, and quite a few of us local chaps went to the funeral. We all rather liked him, you see, and it seemed a shame him having no relatives nor kin to see him decently buried. I'm right sorry, sir; it must have been a bad knock for you."

I had sat as if frozen, my hand still on the half-empty glass, while Jim rambled on. Stat was my friend, the only one I ever had; and I should never hear his slow, quizzical drawl again. . . .

After a little while, I said: "He was in the chair—the one with an antenna on the head-rest?"

"Aye, it had got a queer arrangement of wire on it. Most likely, some of his experiments. Joe told me there was a big, black box underneath, with a generator going in it; he's an electrician, and knows about such things. But with the walls crumbling in hot ashes, and the floor bursting into flames beneath his feet, he didn't waste much time on looking around, as you can guess."

"The motor was going?" I asked, and although I scarcely knew I had spoken, my tone must have startled Jim.

"Why, yes. Leastways, Joe said it was humming, the way they do."

I thanked old Jim, and went outside. For a long time afterwards, I couldn't think straight. First, I went round to the little cemetery of St. Mary's and found Stat's grave. It was marked with a small stone carrying his name and date of death, which some acquaintance had put up; the date was over three weeks ago, I noted. Presently, I walked again up the leaf-strewn lane to the sight of the bungalow, and found myself looking over a heap of ashes. The place had been gutted.

All the time, the horror of it was slowly gathering in my brain, like a storm preparing to burst. I could not rid myself of the remembrance of that sense of disembodiment and eternal aloofness which I had experienced in exploring the past. Words of Stadtland's kept coming back, as I had heard them uttered in that tired drawl:

". . . if that thread were snapped, anything might happen; but it's safe to say it would be nothing pleasant." Again: "I have not found any time limit when the properties of the Time-Drug show signs of weakening."

In the evening, I took rooms at the "Flying Ship." It was there, even the same night that I heard tales of the "appearances," and the "queer doings" up at the bungalow meadow; tales scoffed at, of course, yet "there might be something in it, y'know." Such was the attitude of the bar-parlour. Pressmen, it seemed, and "scientific gentlemen from London," had already been poking around. I listened to it all with the chill hopelessness in my heart deepening.

Next day, I was up at the site of the fire, and the next day—watching, watching, although I never admitted to myself what it was that I was keeping vigil for. It was not until the third day that it appeared, though, round about dusk.

The exact moment of its coming I could not tell, but suddenly I was aware that about six feet above the ground, or about four feet above the level where the floor of the hut had been, hung a vague, half-transparent ovoid. Its colour, if any distinct hue could be made out, was greyish; its shape . . . it had the convolutions, the lobes, a striking resemblance to the human brain.

There was no sound; not the slightest movement or change. It was simply suspended in mid-air. I gazed at it, with despair riving my soul, for an unknown length of time; perhaps half an hour, maybe only a few minutes. Then, without a flicker, it was gone, as a dim light is snapped off by the touch of a switch.

I saw it only twice after that. I settled in Chyne; found a job of sorts, after a while, and spent most of my spare time up by the meadow. What could I have done? Stat, or his body, had been buried a month; the formula, the Drug, the Chair—everything had gone in the fire. I am no chemist; for my life's sake, I could not have reconstructed the formula. Could I go to a chemist, tell him what little I knew, implore him to do something? I should have been counted as insane immediately.

The last recorded "appearance" was two years and four months ago. Since then, though watchers in plenty have looked for it, the "Chyne Apparition" has not been seen again.

But at night, I have bad dreams still, and will always have them, I suppose; dreams in which I am again afloat in the past, and scenes of beauty and agony, of sweetness and terror, unfold and re-unfold ceaselessly. The pageant of earthly and cosmic history is eternally sweeping all around me, while I am something tiny, voiceless, ineffective, forever doomed to witness, but never participate. And oh, God, the loneliness!

When I awake I recall some words of my friend's for comfort:

"*. . . Or, again, in exploring toward the beginning of the universe, one may reach a point of self-annihilation, where the universe first explodes into being . . .*"

Suppose one kept on plunging back—and back—always into the Past . . . . to the beginning of Time . . . ?

Paid without Protest

On the frosted glass of the office door the simple legend, in severely plain black lettering, "M. Voronezh: Financial Advisor," radiated an air of dry, business virtuousness which might well inspire confidence in the bosoms of wavering clients. "Financial Advisor" is so resplendent, and withal so non-committal a term: its resonant syllables may be construed in so many ways and, if you will have it so, cover a multitude of sins.

In the present case, one who knew Mr. Marcus Voronezh would have said unhesitatingly that they stood for moneylender, bucket-shop keeper, patents exploiter, bubble company promoter, small time swindler, confidence man and graft merchant. All of these activities Mr. Voronezh included in his repertoire, together with any others that might offer opportunities for making easy money for a person whose respect for the law extended only beyond the limits at which it could be safely evaded.

At the moment, however, anyone more scrupulous and benign, in outward appearance at least, would have been hard to find.

Mr. Voronezh sat at his neat, maple-wood desk, fingering idly the exquisite white carnation in his lapel and gazing blankly out at a drear vista of empty office windows across the narrow courtyard. Though he gazed, it can scarcely be said that he had any interest in empty offices, or even that he saw them. Inwardly he was filled with the mellow glow of content which comes to one who recounts, mentally, a successful business deal. Already that morning, two useful sums of fifty pounds had enriched his private account.

That both of these were from elderly ladies of slender means in return for shares in a Bolivian tin mine whose worth would have been highly questionable at five shillings caused not twinges at all in Mr. Voronezh's mind. Indeed, if he had thought of them, it would have been with that certain contempt which most pithily expresses itself in the phrase, "Poor suckers!"

The imperative burr of the telephone bell cut into his dreams of rose-and-gold, and recalled him to a world where the demands of business are stern and unremitting. As he placed the receiver to one shell-pink ear, his features and voice alike were bland, courteous and dignified.

"Good morning, Mr. Voronezh," came the disembodied voice over the wires, "my name is Anthony Charles de Palos, and I'm afraid we have never had the pleasure of being acquainted, for regrettable as it is to admit it, it is a name which so far has been the reverse of famous or notorious. I am an inventor, and I have a project which I feel sure will gain your interest and enthusiasm. You do, I believe, occasionally purchase the patent rights in inventions which seem to promise well?"

The voice was young, it was cultured, and had an indefinable, quiet firmness. Not a likeable voice, Marcus decided; he had an inherent dislike of firm, hard young people.

"Why, Mr. de Palos," he replied, "it is true that I have occasionally interested myself in one or two small novelties, but I do not make a practice of it. Purchasing patents is a very risky business in these days, since it by no means follows that a workable idea can be made to catch the public's favour; we have to be perfectly sure, too, that a theoretical idea is practically sound; then again, the cost of popularising and selling an article or process is frequently prohibitive. Just what line does your invention take?"

"You need have no fear, Mr. Voronezhm of this article not proving admirably saleable or practical. Briefly, it may be described as an instrument for obtaining visual as well as audible telephonic communication. By means of a small receiver, which is clipped on to the telephone line, the person who is speaking over the 'phone can gain a perfect view of the one with whom he is conversing, together with his immediate surroundings—"

"My dear young man, are you trying to tell me something about television?" interrupted Marcus sceptically.

"No, no, please do not misunderstand me, Television is a cumbersome and expensive method of seeing at a distance, and embodies a totally different principle. No, this little Phonovisor, as I have termed it, utilises only the minute electrical currents in the telephone, together with the completely new amplifying and scanning method embodied in the receiver case which forms the main secret of the process. It costs no more than a wireless set to run, since it derives its power from dry batteries; it is compact and portable; it can be attached to any telephone, no matter what make; there is only one tuning knob, for adjusting the clarity of vision.

"You can imagine for yourself the value of these Pholovisors on every telephone; they cost roughly three pounds to produce, well within the purchasing power of any home using a 'phone. Anyone who sees one in operation is sure to want to buy; imagine the convenience of friends being able to see each other while talking, to exhibit books, pictures, frocks; the housewife can buy her meat, her confectionary, crockery, linen by seeing them over the 'phone; the—"

"You've no need to tell me what use it would be if there were such an instrument," cut in Voronezh, testily, "but you're not trying to tell me it's a practical proposition, are you?"

"Why, Mr. Voronezh, perhaps you would like a small demonstration? I have of course, my own constructed Phonovisor attached to my telephone here, and if you will permit me to describe what you are wearing. . . . I admire your white carnation for instance, it is a particularly beautiful specimen, and harmonises well with your grey suit and brown-flecked tie. The handkerchief in your breast pocket has a narrow green border, and a little at your right, on the desk, is a small vase of brown chrysanthemums."

Marcus's lower jaw appeared to be suddenly overcome by the effect of gravitation, and his eyes suffered from a peculiar distending. He croaked once or twice.

Suddenly he whipped his fountain pen from the ink-stand and scribbled feverishly and meaninglessly over the desk.

"What am I doing now?" he rasped.

"Why, I'm afraid you're spoiling a perfectly good fountain-pen nib, beside marring the surface of an excellent office desk. Really, you know—"

But Marcus had dropped the telephone and with scarlet face and incoherent vocal noises was rushing about the room as one demented. He ripped a water-colour from the wall, stood it upside-down in a chair and placed a brass ornamental vase before it. Approaching his desk again, he picked up the telephone receiver gingerly as though expecting it to turn and bite him.

De Palos was laughing, coolly and quietly. "A very nice still-life arrangement of the vase, water-colour and chair; reminds me of my art class days when I was very young. Well, Mr. Voronezh, I shall require five thousand pounds for all plans and a model and, on due consideration I am sure you will agree that this is a very modest sum. I will ring you to-morrow at the same time to see if we can make any further arrangements. Think over what I have said. Good-day."

Despite Marcus's frenzied shout there came the click of a replaced receiver, and silence. Hastily he called the exchange.

"Can you trace that call which came through just now, or put me through to the fellow again; I must get hold of that man again. I was not finished."

The voice of the operator was cool and reproving. Perhaps she knew Mr. Voronezh. "I am sorry, but the call was put through on the dial system; we cannot trace that," and the chrysanthemums received the plump man's anguished remarks with an air of shocked reproach.

Mr. Voronezh spent the rest of the day in a state bordering between anxiety, exultation, incredulity and sheer excitement. Fear alternated with hope. If the thing actually worked, were on the level—it couldn't be, of course, but suppose it were; there was a fortune in it, millions. At five thousand it would be dirt cheap. He must have dreamed it—no, he hadn't though; that fellow had described him as if he'd been sitting next to him. He *must* have got something. What of some of those other dam' sharks heard of it, Goldmann, say, or the Castellon gang! Hell, what had the fellow dashed off like that for.

His night was restless and troubled, and he had little refreshing sleep, but in spite of that he was early at his office the next morning and astonished his clerk by saying he was not to be disturbed until he called. At his desk, he fidgeted, watched the clock, attempted to work and cursed nervously.

Promptly at eleven-thirty, however, his vigil was rewarded. As he swooped upon the telephone, something told him that this was the bird he was after.

"Good morning," said a cool, familiar voice in his ear, "I see you are looking well this morning, Mr. Voronezh. You will forgive me if I mention that I rather like the cream-and-blue motif in your tie" (Marcus made a choking sound in his throat.) "However, we must not waste time in pleasantries, for I know you are a busy man and I, too, have my little affairs; I had half arranged to see Messrs. Castellon Brothers this afternoon, over the little novelty I mentioned to you yesterday, but I could not really make it definite until I had had a chat with you. Well, are you at all interested in the proposals? My terms are quite definite and simple; to wit—the sum of five thousand pounds in cash on condition that I hand over to you in your office, plans and a working model of the Phonovisor."

"Let me advise you to keep away from the Castellons, young man," yapped Marcus. "You understand, I have nothing against them personally except that I wouldn't trust them with a baby's money box. And as for paying five thousand pounds for this invention of yours, well that is a ridiculously large sum. The thing certainly interests me, and I might be able to offer you somewhere in the neighbourhood of ten or eleven hundred if I'm satisfied; but even then it's a big risk, for no one can tell whether the public will take to it. There will have to be a company formed, which will take a lot of money; production and advertising will take more. I tell you, I could easily be ruined over this crazy project. I've more than half a mind not to touch it."

"Just as you please, Mr. Voronezh," replied De Palos, calmly; "In that case I will have to say good morning, as I have much business on hand—"

"I said only half a mind," interposed Marcus hastily. "Look here, I'm certainly interested, and I think you'll find I can help you a lot. Bring your plans and the model round to my office and we'll discuss matters more fully. Perhaps I might even make it up to fifteen hundred if the invention seems really good."

"Five thousand, please," answered the cool voice. "I will call on you with the goods at two p.m. precisely. I am a busy man and you will be wasting neither my time nor your own if you have the five thousand ready, in cash. Au revoir."

Mr. Voronezh swore naughtily at the 'phone. This De Palos had a confoundedly annoying habit of making his own arrangements and ringing off at the crucial moments. He did not like people who were independent and made their own terms and stuck to them. It was a pity someone with a little more pliability had not invented the Phonovisor.

Nevertheless, Mr. Voronezh paid a visit to the very discreet and respectable bank with which he did business, and on his return placed a comfortable wad of notes in the strong little wall safe behind the water-colour of pines at Cap Tarifa.

At one forty-five he was back at his maple-wood desk, and thirteen minutes later his clerk ushered in Mr. Anthony Charles de Palos. Marcus noted that he carried under one arm a long black box, of roughly the same shape as a small filing drawer, while the other hand held a worn leather brief case.

De Palos himself might have stood for a physical representation of his voice; young, lean, dark imperturbable, with a certain impassive hardness about the eyes and the corners of his mouth that spoke for no elementary knowledge of the ways of the world.

The preliminaries over, De Palos extracted a bulky sheaf of drawings and manuscripts from the brief case and laid them on the desk. They were technical in the extreme, but as Voronezh glanced through them with an eye long accustomed to patents he saw they represented some form of wiring system and lay-out for high-speed scanning, though the exact details were new and alien to him.

De Palos pointed out certain parts of the apparatus and went into an explanation in technical jargon which was mostly Greek to Mr. Voronezh. "You understand," the young man said, "that it would be foolish for me to explain the basic secret of the process until you have come to a decision, but the whole formulæ and specifications are here in full. Then there is, of course, the full-scale working model of the Phonovisor, which is as good as the plans. You will allow me to demonstrate it to you?"

"Go ahead," said Marcus.

The inventor placed the long, box-like affair on the desk and unrolled from one end two short lengths of copper lead. Scraping a little of the flex from the telephone wires, he clipped these leads securely to them. "A crude method of attachment," he said, with a smile, "but, of course, in future every telephone will be equipped with a simple Phonovisor plug-in connection."

At the end of the box facing Mr. Voronezh was a small screen, some six inches by six, while the upper surface of the case carried merely a switch and a tuning dial. De Palos snapped the switch; the screen glowed dimly white and a faint, musical hum emanated from the instrument.

"Now if you will allow me to use your telephone and call up a friend, we will see what uses the Phonovisor can be put." He handed the extension ear-piece to Marcus, and deftly his slim fingers twirled the dial; May 3202, the watching financier noted.

There came the familiar burr-burr from the 'phone, and after a moment, a click as the receiver was lifted and a girls' voice said "Hallo?" With the click the tiny screen glowed into life, and Mr. Voronezh's eyes again experienced a slight rotundity as he gaped at a perfectly good close-up of a charming face.

"Hello, Pat," said De Palos. "I hope you won't mind doing a small favour for me; I'm demonstrating my Phonovisor to a gentleman here who's interested, and if you could do one or two small things for us, as visual proof so to speak, I'd be frightfully obliged."

The face dimpled and smiled enchantingly. "Why, sure, Tony. Fire away. Thank heaven I tidied my hair before answering, if I'm under observation."

"Vain creature! Well for a start would you mind holding a copy of to-day's paper up to the 'phone?"

The girl disappeared momentarily, and the two men had a view of a small but smartly furnished sitting-room, a flat by appearance.

The young lady appeared again in the field of view, holding a copy of *The Times*, folded so as to bring the date clearly visible; it was Tuesday, the 24th of the month, 193–, the same date as that which stood revealed on Marcus's neat desk calendar,. De Palos let him take a generous look at it.

"O.K., dear. Now if you could take the 'phone over to the clock, please . . . ?"

There was a brief blurring and the scene in the small screen leaped and swung wildly, then they were looking at a diminutive shelf clock whose hands pointed to 2.15 p.m., coinciding almost exactly with those on Mr. Voronezh's wall clock. Again De Palos allowed him to digest the significance.

"Right-ho Pat. And now a glimpse out of your window, if you don't mind."

Again the view of the room did a tango sway, and then Mr. Voronezh's eyes looked down upon a busy street which he knew by sight. Cars passed and re-passed, pedestrians dodged across the road, all in exquisite miniature. It was better than television.

"That will do, I think, Pat. Many thanks for your help; I'll be seeing you later, I expect."

Once again dimpled features gazed out from the screen. "Glad to have been of service, Tony, Say good-bye to your friend for me. Cheerio." With a last smile to which Mr. Voronezh most ungallantly gave no response, the girl vanished and the screen went blank. De Palos touched a switch and the faint humming died into silence.

One thought stood out clear in Marcus's mind like a bright flame; this young man must not be allowed to go out of the room without parting with the Phonovisor, no matter what the cost. He realised as clearly as anything he had ever done that the key to a fortune of the Ford and Rockefeller magnitude lay on his desk. Vague, entrancing visions of himself as Sir Marcus Voronezh, head of a world-wide combine, wielding the power of a modern Napoleon of finance, floated in his mind.

With a magnificent effort he produced his business poker-face, and spoke in a non-committal tone. "Well, Mr. de Palos, you have a useful toy there, but I'm afraid it is little more. Look here, I'll give you fif . . . teen . . . . hundred . . . pounds, cash, on the spot, for it; that is a large sum of money and far more than I ought really to offer. But I like your idea and I'm willing to take a big risk on the chance that I can make some small profit on it."

With a sigh, De Palos shuffled the plans together and began inserting them in the brief case. "A pity. And Mr. Anton Castellon actually suggested three thousand pounds as his first price this morning. Well, I'm sorry . . ."

"Wait a moment," cut in Voronezh, hurriedly. "If that crook, Castellon, offered you three thousand, why hang it! I'll give you the same if it's only to keep you out of his clutches. Three thousand, man, why it's a small fortune!"

"A useful sum, no doubt, but five thousand is my price I am afraid. After all, to anyone who has capital to invest, the invention offers a profit of a hundred times that amount; I have not the capital to exploit it. But I am fully aware that there are many interested parties who would willingly pay the sum, and more, for the Phonovisor."

Mr. Voronezh threw up his hands and silently invoked his ancestors in the face of such obstinacy. "Three thousand, five hundred," he rapped, "and that's my absolute limit. It's idiocy to offer more on a wild gamble."

The inventor hooked up the Phonovisor from the desk and snuggled it in the crook of his arm. "I'm afraid I'll have to be going; honestly, I can't take a pound lower price. We are only wasting time, so I'll have to say good day."

The anguished Marcus grabbed his arm and urged him into a chair. With something approaching a moan he opened the wall-safe and took out the five neatly rubber-banded wads of bank notes which lay there.

At 4.11 precisely, the same afternoon, two thing of interest happened simultaneously.

At Croydon the wheels of a big transcontinental air liner left the ground as the ship climbed slowly heavenward and sent her nose for South Africa. And in Tavis Street, West Central 2, Mr. Voronezh hurled a heavy inkstand through the centre of his discreet, frosted-glass office door.

It was a disgraceful show of temper, of course, but perhaps in the circumstances excusable. For the technical expert with whom he had consulted had pointed out that the detailed and intricate Phonovisor plans were exactly those of a very nice television receiver just come on the market and retailing at twenty-five guineas. Also he found he had purchased a few hundred feet of Cine film portraying an undeniably pretty girl, a *Times*, a clock, and a view of Pennystone Road, with projector and button starting arrangement. The whole was undoubtedly ingeniously constructed and co-ordinated, and would have admirably served the purpose of a Christmas present to a juvenile relation, but perhaps five thousand pounds was a little too steep a price to pay. Mr. Voronezh evidently thought so.

Meanwhile, as the *Carpathia* droned steadily southward above a ceiling cloud Mr. Anthony Roanne and Mrs. Patricia Roanne settled more comfortably into their seats. Mrs. Roanne was jotting down a few financial items in a small notebook.

"Debit—I think that's the correct work, dear—to office rental, ten pounds; living expenses—I think fifteen pounds should clear that.

"Let me see—oh, yes, to Cine camera and projector, plus details of Phonovisor, twenty pounds; to Johnny, for printing that dummy *Times* sheet, two pounds; extras, five pounds, That makes . . . ten, twenty-five, forty-five, seven, fifty-two. On the credit side we have five thousand pounds, leaving, if I am not mistaken, some £4,948 net profit."

"Clever girl," remarked her husband, and offered her a cigarette.

"But you know," she remarked, as she drew daintily at the tobacco, "I think that the thing which really made dear Marcus bite was the groundbait. It was an ingenious idea to rent the empty office over the way and communicate by telephone, while keeping tab on his reactions with the aid of field-glasses."

Sources:

"The Man Who Lived Backwards," *Tales of Wonder* no. 3 (Summer 1938): 22-32.

"The Time-Drug," *Tales of Wonder* no. 5 (Winter 1938): 62-73.

"Paid without Protest," *The Passing Show*, v.7 no. 342 (8 October 1938): 10-12.

Made in the USA
Middletown, DE
31 May 2023

31786484R00031